nickelodeon

The Penguins of Madagascar

DreamWorks

HAPPY KING JULIEN DAY

AND OTHER STORIES

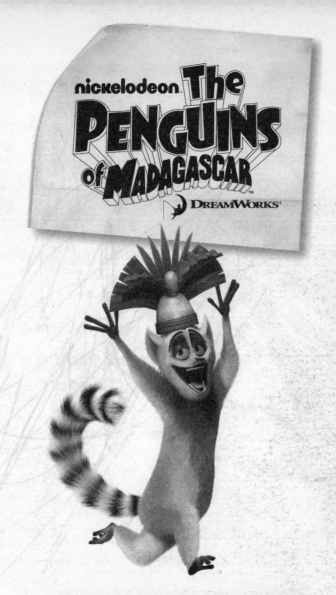

HAPPY KING
JULIEN DAY
AND OTHER STORIES

STORY 1
HAPPY KING JULIEN DAY

It was the middle of the night and the cages of the New York Zoo were all empty. The only sound that could be heard was a mixture of shouting and laughter coming from the Zoovenir shop. All of the animals were assembled, though some more willingly than others, standing amongst the barrels of toys and racks of T-shirts.

Skipper stood to one side, surveying the scene with a watchful eye. "All right," he asked Kowalski, "so, why are we here?"

Kowalski sighed, scratching his chin thoughtfully. "Ahh, the question which has plagued common man and philosopher alike." He glanced down and saw Skipper glaring up at him. Blushing, he said meekly, "That's not what you're going for, is it?"

Private overheard the question and skipped over, saying, "Maurice said he had a very important announcement!"

Skipper groaned.

"All right, might I have everyone's attention?" Maurice commanded from the door. "Everyone?" Maurice shouted even louder. "Eyes and ears? Hello? Is anyone listening?"

But no one paid him any attention.

At that moment, tiny Mort leaped neatly onto Maurice's shoulders, and taking a deep breath yelled, "Quiet!!!"

The animals immediately fell into a shocked silence. Who knew Mort had such big lungs?

Maurice began his speech, "It is my honour to introduce King Julien, leader of lemurs, Lord of the ringtails, etcetera, etcetera, etcetera."

As he spoke, Mort was struggling to push an old-fashioned stereo into the centre of the room. As Maurice finished with a bow, Mort pushed the play button. Right away, the sound of recorded cheers and shouts of praise filled the room and in came King Julien himself, striding confidently through the doors. He paused, pretending to be shocked at the jubilant crowd awaiting him, ignoring the blank stares of the zoo inhabitants and striking a series of poses, his arms raised in greeting and doing the royal wave. Mort quickly paused the stereo and looked up at the King with awe-struck eyes.

King Julien looked down at them all proudly. "Thank you, Maurice," he said loudly, "for your hearty 'etceteras'." Then he turned to the waiting crowd. "I will cut to the chases. In a few hours, we celebrate the biggest holiday of the year!"

Marlene gave a cry of glee and flung her arms into the air, yelling enthusiastically, "Christmas in July!" but soon slumped in disappointment and looked confused. "Except, it's not Christmas. Or July."

King Julien grinned and bent down to whisper in Maurice's large ear. "Look how they playfully tease me, Maurice." He stood up straight and gave them all a knowing wink. "You know I am speaking of King Julien Day! How could you not? It's on every calendar."

Right on cue, Maurice whipped out a souvenir zoo calendar. There was a crudely-drawn picture of King Julien on it.

"What about this one?" Private asked

innocently, making Marlene stifle a laugh at the blank calendar in his flippers.

Julien looked unfazed. Raising an eyebrow, he gestured imperially, "Maurice?"

The obedient lemur quickly scribbled Julien's face all over the calendar page.

"Aha! There it is!" Julien cried, ripping it from Private's clutches and showing it to everyone. "See! So shut up and start shopping!" He turned on his heel and exited the souvenir shop, as Mort replayed the resounding cheers of a pre-recorded crowd. He was the only one clapping.

"So . . . What is King Julien Day?" Marlene questioned, completely puzzled.

Maurice looked around at all the blank faces. None of the animals knew about this holiday. "On King Julien Day, everybody loads up the gifts on the King and pretty much does whatever he says." When he saw that no one looked as excited as they should, he promised, "It's eight kinds of fun, no lies," trying, but failing, to look believable.

"I see . . . In that case," Skipper said, making fun of Maurice's fake enthusiasm, before crossing his flippers sternly. "Pass!"

All the zoo animals started to leave, uninterested in King Julien Day. Maurice panicked as they filed past him.

"Listen to me!" he cried in desperation. "You don't understand this here situation! Trust me, you want King Julien to be happy on his holiday!"

The animals paused, curious. He shuddered, recalling the horrible memory of King Julien gazing sternly at his subjects with thunder cracking all around them, a bamboo held aloft in his hands, shouting, "Which forgetter is next for their whooping? Come on! I want you to hurt like I do." After reliving one of the most terrifying moments of his life, Maurice looked shaken.

"The one time everyone forgot about King Julien Day . . . well, let's just say I couldn't sit right for a week!" He rubbed his backside as the memory continued to haunt him. "Trust me, you do NOT want him to freak out on you."

Skipper chuckled at the idea that any ring-tailed lemur could stand a chance against his team's superior martial arts skills. "We'll take our chances."

But before they could leave, Mort leapt bravely in front of them, blocking the door, begging, "Please! King Julien Day is my favourite holiday in the whole wide world!" He spread his arms as wide as he could reach. "I love it this much!"

Kowalski tipped his head to one side and surveyed the small mammal before him. "That's a lot of love relative to body mass," he said, but still reached for the door handle.

"Whoa! Just hold up!" Maurice yelled, getting desperate. "Does anyone remember that kid's birthday party here last week?"

Phil expertly signed to Mason in their primate code and Mason nodded, "Ah, yes, poor little chap's party got rained out."

"Well," said Maurice, practically glowing with pride. "When the humans ran for cover, Mort and I snatched this!" He pulled out a tattered horse-shaped piñata from behind a crate and wielded it like a weapon. No one knew what it was, not even Kowalski, so Maurice gave a smug grin. "Do you know what the people put in these things?" He paused, seeing Private alight with curiosity. "Candy. Lots of it!"

Seven jaws dropped with a collective gasp and for the first time that night, Maurice held a captive audience. He rattled the piñata enticingly.

Kowalski leaned forward, his eyes wide with disbelief, muttering to himself. "The forbidden fruit-flavoured food."

Marlene was thrilled and said in a crazed voice, "I want to crack it open on my belly and dig out the creamy centre. Yum!" She began to mime eating the sweets, completely absorbed in her dreams of an unending supply of sugared treats.

"That's right, this piñata is full of sweet deliciousness," Maurice said, knowing that there was only one way to persuade the reluctant zoo animals to help, and it was encased inside the papier-mâché horse. As he rattled it for the second time, one lonely sweet fell out and rolled across the floor.

"Mmm-mmm. What have we here?" Maurice said, pretending to be curious.

Nine pairs of eyes followed it, hungrily, but Maurice was quick to snatch it up and tear off the purple wrapping, before crunching it between his teeth. He patted his stomach, looking satisfied, as Marlene grumbled that it was not fair.

"Lots more where this came from," he told the gang of hungry penguins, monkeys and otters. "They'll all be yours . . . if y'all just celebrate King Julien Day like you mean it."

Unfortunately, the ravenous Rico was not in the mood to wait. He whipped out his baseball bat, which he always kept on his person in case of such situations. He jumped into the air, ready to perform a perfectly executed swing at the piñata, but Maurice managed to pull it out of the way, just in time.

Rico's bat smashed into Mort, who went flying out of the highest window, his scream fading into the night as Rico stowed his bat away guiltily.

The next day, the penguins were holding their daily meeting. Skipper surveyed the preparations for King Julien Day through his prized periscope, muttering to himself. "Maurice thinks he can bribe us with piñata promises. But sadly for him, penguins are not for sale. Right, men?"

He turned to his team, who were assembled around the meeting table, talking animatedly about the very piñata promises that Skipper was so scornful of.

"What do you think is in there? I think there are butterscotch lollipops and sourballs," Private said dreamily, whilst Kowalski pondered the question. He came to a conclusion.

"I'd say we're looking at a 50/50 mixture of gummy fish and candy buttons."

Rico almost fainted at the mention of his favourite chocolate sweet, his tongue lolling over the side of his beak.

Skipper thought it was high time to end this before it got out of hand. "We may never know, because tonight we're performing scheduled maintenance on the HQ."

Kowalski, Private and Rico were grief-stricken, unable to decide whether or not to disobey their leader. How could they pass up sweets?

"Perhaps we could postpone?" Kowalski mentioned timidly, thinking about how long it had been since he had eaten a gummy fish.

Skipper glared and replied, "Negative. You can't just reschedule 'scheduled' maintenance. Which has been scheduled, right on the schedule."

Private felt bad. "Skipper is right," he argued. "Candy is candy." He blinked, realizing what he had said and added hastily, "I mean, duty is duty."

Kowalski and Rico hung their heads in sorrow and agreement. Skipper thought they looked like the most forlorn penguins who ever lived. He smiled and accepted defeat. "Shore leave granted for tonight, men, now get out of here, you bunch of knuckleheads."

Private jumped up and rushed over to hug the generous penguin.

One hour later, King Julien stood tall on his bamboo throne, glancing over the enclosure and searching for signs of life.

"Where are my guests? Come out, come out, wherever you are!" King Julien called in a singsong voice. "It is time to celebrate me and the many moods of me! Tonight: festive me!"

He slid off his chair and onto the ground, but immediately had to jump from foot to foot as an over-excited Mort danced around him in circles crying, "King Julien Day! King Julien Day!" at the top of his lungs.

Just then, Mason, Phil and Marlene entered the pen, carrying flowers and huge bunches of bananas. Mason cleared his throat, announcing their arrival. "We're here for the candy," he coughed to hide his mistake. "I mean the party, of course."

At that moment, Private, Kowalski and Rico arrived to join the festivities.

King Julien looked at his guests with pure happiness and bellowed, "Welcome, my loyal royal subjects!"

There was silence, until Maurice quickly held the hidden piñata aloft and Marlene yelled, excitedly, "Happy King Julien Day." She knew that sweets came before pride.

King Julien nodded his head in approval, "See, the otter is in the holiday spirit."

It was time to get into his holiday spirit, so Julien nodded regally at his lemur aide.

Maurice cleared his throat, and spoke through a rolled-up palm megaphone, "Everyone, now bask in the glory that is King Julien!"

The King in question grinned widely – this was the best part of being King, when people recognized his superiority.

"Go ahead, bask!" he said contentedly, and the animals looked at each other with raised eyebrows, before remembering Maurice's bribe. They changed their sceptical looks to looks of awe, pretending to be mightily impressed by the self-important lemur. "Oooh," they cried, and "Aaah."

King Julien jumped up and down, punching his fists in the air. "Bask harder!" he cried, as Maurice waved the sweet-stuffed piñata behind him.

"Oh! Ah! Oh! Ah!" the animals shouted, basking harder than they had ever basked before, throwing their gifts onto the royal platform.

Julien clapped his hands together and pointed down at the jubilant crowd beneath him, "Now, just the fellas!"

Private, Rico, Kowalski and Mason cheered loudly, as Phil mimed animatedly.

"Ladies!' Julien ordered next, leaving a lone Marlene awkwardly basking by herself.

"A-ah?" she said quietly, blushing.

King Julien's right eye began to twitch slightly, his head jerking in random movements as he clenched his teeth in rage. "Hmmm, the ladies sound a little weak; you know how that makes me, Maurice."

Maurice knew he had to act fast, so he raised the rolled-up palm leaf megaphone, shouting, "Now let's get this party started! Everybody, let's limbo!"

Many years in the service of the lemur king had taught him that a distracted Julien was a happy Julien, and limbo was the best distraction possible.

Mort wobbled over, nearly breaking under the weight of a large limbo stick and Maurice banged the old stereo to force it to play a jaunty tropical tune. Marlene was the first to squeeze under the pole, nearly falling over as she lost her balance, flinging herself forward far enough to clear the pole and land in a heap. "Must have candy," she panted, as she rubbed her back in agony.

"Now I will make you all feel inferior. Which is proper," Julien cheered, as he started his limbo turn. He stood a few paces away from the limbo pole, which was now only a few inches off the ground, flexing his legs and doing a series of stretches. He ran up to the pole and tipped himself so that he was completely horizontal, walking only on the edge of his toes. The zoo animals were in amazement, having never seen such a feat of limbo achievement in their lives.

"Yes! Did you see?" Julien boasted, I am not only the King, but I am also the Limbo King, too!"

Marlene grumbled to herself. She would like to see him try to swim, but before she could voice her opinion, Maurice said in an official-sounding voice, "King Julien wins the limbo contest!"

"Thank you for your boisterous and loving cheers," Julien crooned at the animals, who were all glaring directly at him. "Hello?" he tried again. "New York, put your hands or other appendages together now," he pointed at them aggressively until he got a small applause.

Maurice rubbed his eyes in exasperation.

"Next . . .The traditional King Julien Day tossing of the fruit!"

Private blinked, completely bemused at this next crazy plan.

"The tossing of the fruit?" Marlene asked with equal befuddlement, "Tossing it where, exactly?"

Before she could even begin to speculate, half a melon hit her squarely in the face and she flew back with an "Omff!"

Maurice smiled, sympathetically.

"At you . . . Exactly," he said, leaning over her, seeing the pieces of melon that were stuck to her brown fur.

"At us?" Kowalski echoed, turning away in disapproval. "No!"

At this, King Julien quickly turned around and glared straight at Kowalski, his eye starting to twitch slightly yet again. "Did I hear somebody say, 'No'?"

Maurice panicked and looked at Kowalski, his eyes wide in terror, drawing his hand across his neck to mimic the terrible outcome if Julien was disobeyed on his holiday. He secretly showed the piñata again to help remind Kowalski of the task at hand.

"Mmm . . . chewy centre. Yo, I am down with that!" Kowalski exclaimed, faking enthusiasm.

Kowalski's face went slack, as his mind drifted to the gummy fish and chocolate buttons.

Julien paused to consider, before stating, "Then let the fruit fight begin!" He raised a giant pineapple over his head, lobbing it with all his

strength at Rico and quickly throwing great piles of fruit at them, one after the other. They all tried to run and hide, but Julien was watching them with an eagle eye. Even the expertly-trained penguins felt terror seize them, as they legged it around the enclosure, trying to avoid being turned into a fruit smoothie.

King Julien was having the time of his life.

"Yes!" he cheered. "You love getting hit with my unripe fruit! I can tell by your screams."

Over in the penguin HQ, Skipper had resorted to wearing a big pair of fluffy earmuffs in order to drown out the party sounds and jungle music that was leaking in through the windows. He had just completed the finishing touches on his periscope. All the grime of use had gone and it was shinier than it was when Kowalski had first built it. He nodded in approval, "Nothing more satisfying than a job well done."

No sooner had he finished his sentence than a melon missile hit the lens of the periscope and exploded everywhere. At once, Skipper went into fight mode and yelled to no one in particular, "I just cleaned that!"

He jumped out of HQ with a perfectly balanced back flip and landed in a battle stance. Looking behind him for intruders, he failed to see the grapefruit hurtling towards him at breakneck speed. With a mighty CRASH! he fell to the floor.

After struggling for a few moments to regain both his pride and his breath, he slowly stood up. His gaze fell on King Julien, who was dancing

on top of a mound of fruit, gleefully throwing it in all directions. Skipper glared at him, but seeing another piece of fruit heading his way, he ducked and quickly decided to return back underground to work on a strategy.

At the party, the fruit-throwing extravaganza was over, and Julien was back on his throne, the only one who was not dripping with mushy fruit.

Maurice stood below him, holding a giant clipboard, looking down at the exasperated animals, saying, "Now where was I? Oh, yeah – it's time for the bake-off! You have one hour to bake the King the best King Julien Day cake ever . . ."

"Because what is a party without a cake?" Julien wisely pondered, before rubbing his chin thoughtfully. "Well, it's still a party I suppose, but it feels like something is missing . . ." He clicked his fingers, as the answer suddenly came to him, "Something cakey."

"Um . . . Does anyone here know how to bake?" Marlene said, looking around worriedly as the rest of the gang shook their heads.

"Why are they shaking when they are supposed to be baking, Maurice?" asked King Julien, unable to understand why they were not already busy baking for him.

"That's not what they're saying," Maurice said, trying to sound confident. But King Julien could not be fooled, at least not this time. "I think they are. And I am about to freak on them," he threatened, beginning to shake, his eyes rolling wildly.

"Oh, here it comes! The freak out!" Maurice was getting tired of how much encouragement these animals needed to make this holiday a happy one for King Julien. He again dragged out the piñata, pointing to it and then to his stomach emphatically until they all jumped to attention.

"Then again," Private said quickly, "I've always wanted to learn baking." The promise of sweets worked again.

Maurice slumped in relief. "See," he told Julien, soothingly, "no need to freak," before bellowing to the others, "The bake-off starts NOW!"

They all quickly scattered, racing through the zoo in search of any ingredients that they could use. The penguins had dashed back to the lair and Kowalski had quickly calculated some complicated diagrams and algebraic formula to help construct the most mathematically perfect cake ever. Mason and Phil just mashed up all their ingredients on a stone slab, whilst Marlene stirred manically, thinking only of the sweets that awaited her at the end of the day.

Time flew, faces were covered with flour, paws and flippers ached from smoothing layers of icing and by the end there was a lot of burnt fur and feathers.

PING! Time was up, and Maurice called for all the animals to re-enter the enclosure and present the cakes to the King. Marlene was the first to approach, with a sloppy cake lathered in white icing, dotted with a few bugs and pieces of fruit.

"Very nice. Do I see bugs in there?" King Julien asked curiously, leaning in to see the little insects crawling and slithering through the icing.

Marlene gulped nervously. "Lemurs love bugs, right?" She picked up a startled Mort and abruptly shook him over the cake, letting all his fleas and ticks fall over her hard work.

Julien nodded, "Ordinarily yes, but I am on a low-tick diet." With one sweeping hand gesture, Maurice bundled her off to the side.

Next up were Mason and Phil, holding something that looked suspiciously like a pineapple carved into a cake-like shape with the leaves hanging off the bottom. Phil began to sign, and Mason looked at him before translating, "Pineapple upside-down cake. Glazed with brown booger." Phil hit him over the head furiously and corrected him. "My mistake," Mason said, "brown sugar."

King Julien did not look convinced and glanced at the cake with trepidation, "Eh . . . just in case," he turned to Maurice and shook his head, "Next!"

The three penguins waddled proudly in front of the King, carrying a stick of dynamite jammed into the middle of what looked like a vast chocolate cake. Just as the dynamite was about to go off, Kowalski blew it out, glaring angrily at Rico who shrugged and tried to look innocent.

"Death by Chocolate," Kowalski announced, as the King leaned forward to inspect the cake.

"Ooh," Julien marvelled, "the chocolate part sounds promising."

"We didn't exactly have chocolate as such," Private admitted, quietly.

Julien looked at it wearily and asked, "What did you have?"

"Mainly mud," replied Kowalski.

King Julien beamed and stretched out his hands towards it. "Nice presentation. Bring it so that my belly may taste its yumminess."

"I'll bring it!" squeaked Mort excitedly, scurrying over and taking the cake from Private, raising it high above his head as he struggled to totter over to Julien.

Suddenly, Mort's foot got trapped under a bamboo mat and . . . CRASH! He was flung face first onto the floor as the cake soared out of his hands and over the fence.

Unknown to the party, it landed right on Skipper's head as he brushed the final piece of melon off his periscope.

"Urgh!" Julien cried. "I was so looking forward to eating my delicious cake."

He clutched his head and shook it from side to side, crying over the unfairness of it all. "How can I look forward to eating nothing?" He picked up and shook his closest advisor. "Answer me, Maurice!"

Maurice was very nervous indeed, and struggled to find an answer. "They'll make new cakes," he answered, hoping that they still wanted the piñata enough to repeat the torture of the last hour, as he grabbed his megaphone,

"New bake-off, on the double!"

Before the animals could make even the slightest sound of agreement or anger at this proposal, an angry penguin arrived with 'Death by Chocolate' perched perilously on his head, looking like an edible but unstylish hat.

"Hold it, party boy!" he ordered, pointing angrily at the lemur on the throne, talking in a low and menacing voice. "A quiet night of routine lair maintenance. Is that too much to ask? Is it?" The anger in Skipper's voice put all the animals on edge, and Mort ran behind Maurice for protection.

"I don't know," the tiny lemur cried, terror piercing his tone.

Skipper continued, "You bombard me with music and fruit and this!" he pointed to the cake, which was dripping over his scowling face. "Newsflash lower mammal – there is no such thing as King Julien Day!"

There was a stunned silence and Maurice could not dare to look at his king, frozen with horror at the thought of a freak-out of the same magnitude as the last. Mort fainted in fright and the others let out a collective gasp, as King Julien leaned forward, his eyes wild and his hands raised as though ready to strike. His lip trembled and he looked as though he was about to burst as he exclaimed, "My cake is back! It's my cake everybody! It came back!" snatching it off Skipper's head and jumping around in glee. He leapt off his throne and stood in front of Skipper, rapping him hard on the hand and chortling, "Silly penguin. Have some in your head, not on it!"

Julien turned to Maurice and said, "I am thinking that this was the best King Julien Day ever."

Maurice let out a sigh of relief, happy that the whole ordeal was over. "I think so too."

As Julien bounded off to feast on his cake, Skipper muttered, "Sicko!"

Almost dizzy with happiness, Maurice replied, "Tell me about it. You saved my big old behind, Skipper. And you earned this crew one big old piñata."

Marlene, the chimps and the other penguins cheered louder than they had the entire day.

"Bang-up job, Skipper. I can almost taste that butterscotch lolly!" Private complimented his leader happily, as Maurice brought out the piñata. He was just about to hand it over to the drooling zoo animals when Julien popped up out of nowhere, a ring of icing adorning his face.

"What do we have here?" he questioned curiously, looking at the colourful papier-mâché horse with wonder. He grabbed the piñata, hopping up and down. "A big paper horse? How did you know that this is the present I have always wanted? I will name him Bob," he decided firmly, gazing at his new gift with adoration. He jumped onto Bob's back and patted his nose gently.

"Um," Maurice stalled, thinking of a way to break the news to King Julien, rubbing his hands together, nervously. "Your Majesty, that's actually a piñata."

"A pin-whata? Why are you making up words, Maurice?" Julien said, before turning his attention back to the pink and blue horse. "Come, Bob, let me show you around." And with that, he happily bounced off into the distance on his new birthday present.

Marlene and the others could not have looked more downcast if they tried. She blinked back tears, saying, "But . . . our sweets," in a broken voice. Maurice looked on, trying hard to fight the great surge of guilt that came over him as he watched Private trying to comfort Rico and Phil, who was too upset to sign.

They heard a strange bouncing noise and all looked up to see King Julien come trotting back on Bob, unable to tear their eyes away from their lost sweets.

"Silly King me!" he said, wagging a finger at himself in mock seriousness, "I almost forgot the traditional sharing of the sweets."

Everyone looked up, hope shining in their eyes, as he continued rambling, "And wouldn't you know, Bob has candy guts!"

Julien slid off his horse and made a rip in Bob's backside. At once, a vast array of chocolate, butterscotch lollies, buttons and gummy fish fell out, covering the ground with forbidden treats.

"Dig in!' the King said happily, and at once Marlene, Mason, Phil, Kowalski, Private and Rico started to attack the pile ravenously, stuffing their faces with confectionery until their teeth were stuck together with toffee and they could no longer talk.

Julien looked on, his hands clasped to his chest, and smiled brightly. "Go on!" he said, "enjoy Bob's guts on me."

King Julien Day actually turned out to be a pretty happy day for everyone, after all!

STORY 2
GONE IN A FLASH

In the lemur habitat, Maurice was busily preparing a huge ice cream, excitedly bobbing up and down and singing to himself, "Making my ice cream, ooh-ooh, sprinklin' it up!" He dropped great mounds of toppings onto the treat. He surveyed his work, trying to figure out what was missing from the perfect dessert. "Woo!" He had it! He bent down behind the bar.

King Julien wandered over to the bar, gazing at the ice cream hungrily and licking his lips in anticipation.

As Maurice turned away from his yummy ice cream creation, Julien quickly snatched the sundae and ate it all in a single bite.

Maurice stood up triumphantly. "Now we're addin' a cherry on top!" he sang, and went to place it on the crest of the delicious treat . . . but it had vanished! The paper bowl was resting on the bar top, but not a single drop was left inside for the famished lemur.

Maurice was speechless, as Julien pinched the cherry from between his fingers and gobbled that too.

"Less sprinkles next time, OK, Maurice?" he ordered.

Later that afternoon, Maurice's high spirits were restored. The sun was shining and he had decided to indulge in a spot of relaxation. He had already carefully positioned a sun-lounger in the shade, where he could keep cool and doze.

Now he moseyed towards it and sung to himself, "Gonna relax, mmm-mmm, take a load off!"

He closed his eyes, lifted his bottom into the air and sat down with a bump! "Ow!" he screeched in shock. Julien had snatched the lounger out from under him.

"The sun is much sunnier over here," Julien advised, as he stretched out contentedly on the chair and let out a huge yawn. Maurice growled.

The old lemur stormed off to the opposite end of the enclosure and sat sulking, before taking out his last banana and looking around suspiciously. He was determined to enjoy this treat.

"Wanna eat my banana . . . hope no one TAKES IT!" he sang, whilst searching for the telltale signs that King Julien was following him. Satisfied that he was finally alone, he slowly peeled it, grinned to himself, and closed his eyes as he went to take a huge bite . . . but the only thing that he ended up biting was his tongue.

Maurice let out a feral, angry growl when he saw King Julien perched on a rock above him, licking each of his fingers and rubbing his tummy happily. He'd pinched his food again!

"Nicely done Maurice, now peel me a grape."

"But that was –" Maurice began to protest.

"'Grape', Maurice, 'grape' – not 'lip'!" Julien interrupted.

Maurice snarled with pent-up rage, but said nothing. He knew better than to try and argue with Julien. Rule number one: You do not question the King.

Over in the monkey enclosure, Mason and Phil were busy messing around with a camera they had stolen from a tourist. They were having great fun posing and taking pictures, but soon saw the zookeeper, Alice, approaching their pen. The tourist was walking with her, searching the ground frantically.

"Here's where I last had the camera – it couldn't just disappear!" he exclaimed, scratching his head.

Panicking, Mason thrust the camera into Phil's hands as Alice peered into the enclosure. The monkeys tossed the camera back and forth a few times, neither wanting to get caught red-handed, before Phil finally chucked it over his shoulder. It soared over the fence and landed in Maurice's arms, as he stood listening to yet another lecture from Julien.

"Oooh, I'll take that!" screeched Julien when he spotted it.

Meanwhile, in the penguin enclosure, Skipper, Kowalski, Private and Rico were relaxing by the pool and slurping Private's special sardine smoothie. Kowalski was holding a metallic sun reflector under his chin, hoping to get a nice colour. The penguins were on a rare day off, when no hare-brained scheme had been concocted and there were no missions to complete.

"Private, these sardine smoothies are really top-notch," said Skipper, appreciatively. "What's your secret?"

"Love, Sir. I made them with love . . ." Private said sweetly, stroking his cup.

"Love?" asked Skipper, not understanding.

"It's a chemical reaction in the brain inducing bliss. Highly addictive," Kowalski explained knowledgeably.

Skipper quickly tipped the rest of his smoothie onto the ground. He was a penguin, not a kitten!

"No more 'love' in the smoothies, troops. We've got to stay sharp." Skipper narrowed his eyes and his voice became very serious. "The concrete jungle is an elusive mistress who may call us to action at any moment!"

Right on cue, the penguins heard shouts coming from the lemur pen.

"Gimme, gimme, GIMME!" King Julien yelled, as he tried to wrestle the camera from a determined Maurice. Neither lemur knew what a camera was, of course, but they were still entranced by its mystery.

"I said 'gimme'! What part of 'gim' and 'me' do you not understand?" Julien demanded as he and Maurice battled over the camera.

"I understood the 'me' part. Like, this was caught by *me*!" Maurice exclaimed.

Maurice had decided it was time to stand up to Julien – after he'd stolen his ice cream, sun-lounger and then his banana, he was definitely not going to get his hands on this magic box. Both lemurs narrowed their eyes in determination and commenced a tug-of-war. King Julien pulled and pulled at the camera, trying to throw Maurice off balance – but the old lemur had cunningly dug his heels into the earth and was simply unmoveable.

As King Julien gave one final tug, gritting his teeth in anger, one of his hands slipped. Not wanting to lose his grip, he clamped his hand down on top of the camera, accidentally pressing the shutter release button. There was a burst of white light as the flash fired into action, and both lemurs stumbled backwards in shock.

Maurice staggered around, veering close to the edge of the rock they were standing on, until he lost his balance entirely and tumbled over, disappearing completely from sight.

Julien landed safely, but was temporarily blinded by the flash and hadn't seen Maurice's fall. He sat up groggily, rubbed his eyes with his tail and looked around him. After a few moments he realized that there was something missing. To be more precise, Maurice was missing.

"Maurice? . . . Maurice?" he called. "Where are you and your booty, which is quite large and usually easy to see?"

But King Julien could not see Maurice's booty anywhere. He was bending to look over the edge of the rock when he heard a terrified scream. He turned to find Mort shaking in front of the camera.

"Mort, do not scream at my –" he began, marching over to reprimand the little lemur, but stopped in his tracks when he saw what had scared him.

"Waaah!" screeched Julien.

On the camera's digital display screen was a picture of Maurice, his eyes wide and his mouth

gaping with shock – Julien had taken a picture of him as he'd fallen backwards!

Mort lifted one shaking arm and pointed towards the camera. "Maurice! H-h-he's trapped!"

The lemurs still hadn't grasped the basic function of the camera. They really believed Maurice had been caught inside when the flash had gone off.

Julien picked it up and peered fearfully into the display. He shrugged sheepishly, as he racked his brains to find an excuse. He knew Maurice's predicament was his fault, but he certainly wasn't going to take responsibility for it.

"Oh, uh . . . well, yes . . . that is what happens when you question your king's power!" he said with authority.

"I question nothing!" Mort cheeped, lovingly. He was clutching Julien's feet, his eyes wide with admiration.

"I question why you touch the feet!" Julien bellowed, kicking him skywards.

He looked at the camera again and pointed a finger smugly at the screen. "What have you got to say for yourself now, Maurice?!"

No response.

Julien held the camera at arms-length and looked at Maurice, frozen in his expression of fear. A slow smile crept across his face and he nodded his head, knowingly.

"Ah! You are giving to me the 'silent treatment'!" he laughed.

Still no answer.

Julien frowned.

42

"You think this no-talky stuff will get to me?"

Now he was annoyed. He wasn't going to let Maurice win this fight, either. "Forget it, Maurice, I also can give you 'the treatment'." He placed the camera down and sat with his back to it, his arms crossed, determined to be silent.

"Talking to a camera?" scorned Skipper.

The penguins had entered the enclosure and were watching the spectacle with amusement. "This is not normal." He rolled his eyes. What was Julien up to now?

"No, no! No more talky!" barked Julien, pointing at the camera, his eyes fixed and determined. "I am giving him the 'shhh' treatment."

"What, the camera?" asked Kowalski, puzzled.

"No. Maurice," said Julien.

"The ca-me-ra," said Skipper, slowly and carefully, pointing at it. This lemur was really dense – he was going to have to spell it out for him.

"No, Mauuuu-riiiice," replied Julien in the same tone, pointing at the image on the screen. Why couldn't they see that he was locked inside? He walked over to the camera and picked it up – he was going to have to explain what had happened to these silly penguins. "Maurice questioned my kingly authority! So now, he is trapped inside this magic thingy, which the sky spirits gifted to me – the King – from above. Up there." He finished his explanation by raising his arms to the sky, awestruck.

Skipper sighed and walked over to it. "It's not magic," he explained slowly, "it's a camera.

Let me show you."

He reached to take it from Julien, but the lemur held it out of reach, protectively.

"It is a magic king thing! Which you will not touch! Do you want to join Maurice in there? Just try me! Make my day, mister . . ."

"All right, boys," Skipper scoffed, walking away, "let's leave the mad man to his madness."

But before he could take another step, he felt something tugging on his flipper. Mort was clinging onto him in desperation, his large brown eyes glinting pleadingly.

"Spit it out, sad eyes," Skipper said, trying to sound as comforting as he could, which was not very comforting at all.

Tears welled up in Mort's eyes and he sniffed sadly before speaking. "The King's giving Maurice –" He paused and looked around furtively, afraid that he would be overhead. "The 'treatment'. He's going to leave him in the magic box. You have to help him get out!"

Skipper patted Mort's head, patronisingly.

"Your lower-mammal brains don't seem to comprende: that is a camera and your little pal is NOT in it."

"But, Skipper," Private offered, his head to one side, "if Maurice isn't here . . . where is he?"

Skipper gasped. "He must be missing!"

He thrust his flipper into the air in excitement and switched immediately into high-speed, super-efficient operation-mode. "Kowalski: your thoughts?"

Kowalski whipped out his white board and

began to do what seemed like very quick but very complicated calculations. His pen squeaked as it flew across the board and he finally cleared his throat to deliver the verdict.

"I suggest we enlist Doris the dolphin to use her echo-location skills to track the missing lemur." He turned the board dramatically to demonstrate his theory, revealing a really rather simplistic diagram of a dolphin, a lemur, and a couple of arrows. A child could have done it.

"Forget it! She's useless on land," said Skipper, dismissively. "Besides, she might like you, Kowalski, but she doesn't 'like you' like you." Kowalski cast his eyes down in disappointment. "Now!" barked Skipper enthusiastically. "Let's crack this mystery wide open . . ."

The penguins sprang into action, scouring the entire area for clues. Private searched the ground but only found some lint, and Rico might have discovered a major lead in the form of a half-eaten banana if only he hadn't gobbled it up.

"Hey mister, that's evidence!" shouted Skipper.

Kowalski was too busy sighing over a framed picture of Doris the dolphin and sipping on another sardine smoothie to join in.

"Kowalski, I said lay off the love smoothies!" barked Skipper.

Suddenly, he caught sight of some strange marks through his magnifying glass. His eyes narrowed as he looked at the black scratches on the lemur rock and his mind searched for an explanation.

"Scuff marks from a portly lemur," he

murmured. "My guess . . . he stumbled backwards. But why?"

The others crowded round in interest. "Perhaps a localized seismic event of unknown origin," deduced Kowalski.

Private jumped excitedly – he had an idea. "Or maybe the camera's flash blinded him!" he offered.

"Sounds a little preposterous, Private," said Skipper, sceptically. He thought for a moment and rubbed his chin with his flipper. "But just in case . . . Kowalski: run a temporarily-blinded-portly-lemur scenario!'

Kowalski jumped to attention. "Stand right here, Rico," he said, pushing the penguin to the edge of the rock. He whipped out his white board again and started calculating furiously. "Uh-huh . . . mmm-mmm," he mused as he worked, "carry the one . . . ooh!"

He clipped the pen to the top of the board in a gesture of finality. But instead of announcing a solution, he simply thwacked Rico over the precipice, who fell, sprung off the lemurs' bouncy castle and plunged headlong into a rubbish bin just outside the enclosure.

Skipper leapt onto the bouncy castle and flew over the fence. The three penguins landed neatly beside the rubbish bin as Rico popped up with an empty polystyrene cup perched on his head.

"That confirms our target landed in this waste receptacle," Kowalski said. But Maurice was nowhere in sight.

HAPPY KING JULIEN DAY

THE TRADITIONAL KING JULIEN DAY THROWING OF THE FRUITS...AT YOU!

BASK IN THE GLORY THAT IS KING JULIEN.

KING JULIEN DEMANDS YOU BASK HARDER.

EVERYONE PRETENDED TO BASK, BECAUSE THE LEMURS PROMISED CANDY.

"DEATH BY CHOCOLATE CAKE"- PENGUIN STYLE.

A SWEET ENDING TO KING JULIEN DAY.

GONE IN A FLASH

MMM...SARDINE SMOOTHIES.

KING JULIEN'S BIG-BOOTIED BUDDY MAURICE DOES WHAT HE COMMANDS.

TRAPPED!

THE PENGUINS EXPLAIN THAT IT'S A CAMERA, BUT KING JULIEN DOESN'T BELIEVE THEM.

LOOKS LIKE ANOTHER MISSION FOR THE PENGUINS.

MAURICE DECIDES THAT MAYBE KING JULIEN ISN'T SO BAD AFTER ALL.

LAUNCHTiME

PRIVATE SUGGESTED THE PENGUINS GO ON HOLIDAY AT A ZOO - ANOTHER ZOO.

PENGUIN MISSION TO THE MOON!

THE MOON LOOKS SIMILAR TO NEW YORK.

BEING ON THE MOON MAKES THE PENGUINS THINK ABOUT THEIR LEMUR NEIGHBOURS AT HOME.

THE PENGUINS GIVE A TIN OF SARDINES TO THEIR MOON CAT FRIEND.

BLAST OFF!

At that moment, the penguins spotted a human on the path, who was emptying all of the rubbish bins into a large container.

"Ah ha! I know exactly what happened. Into the can, men," commanded Skipper.

The penguins did a back flip into the bin, one by one, in the nick of time. The man scooped the bin out of its holder and emptied all the rubbish, and the penguins with it, into his wheelie dumpster. They were heading out of the zoo!

Later that night, the mass of rubbish from the zoo reached its destination – the dump. The garbage was piled so high that if you stood on the very top, you would have been as tall as the skyscrapers of New York. Night had fallen and it was peaceful, the only sound the scuttle of rats crawling around the waste. At least it *was* a peaceful night, until the lid of a broken toilet seat popped open to reveal Private, looking a little confused. In the same instant, Rico's head broke through a cardboard box, a lightbulb clamped between his teeth, and Skipper exploded from the top of a Jack-in-the-box.

"Kowalski?" Skipper called out searchingly. "Coordinates?"

An abandoned guitar case opened up beside him. Kowalski was inside clutching an old car number plate.

"New Jersey," he deduced, reading from the plate.

"Ahhh . . ." sighed Skipper, breathing in the rotten aroma, dreamily. "The Garden State. I wish we had time to play tourist . . ." He snapped back into action. "All right! We're gonna search this dump high and low, from the rusted tin cans –"

"Skipper! Over here!" interrupted Private, who was standing on top of a large heap, pointing at Maurice. So much for Skipper's grand speech.

Maurice had built himself a rickety shelter made from something that looked like a broken umbrella, propped up with a musty mop. He was stirring a can of mouldy baked beans with a stick, as Skipper approached him triumphantly. Maurice looked horrified.

"What? How did you get here?" he said, frowning angrily.

"Nice work, Private. Happy ending!" Skipper said, extending a flipper to the sky, ready and waiting for a high-five.

But Maurice had his arms tightly folded and just stared at him, grim-faced. Not quite the reception Skipper was expecting.

"Come on, Maurice!" Skipper said, jovially. "Don't leave me hanging!"

"What are you doing here?" he asked gruffly.

"We're here to rescue you!" said Private.

"You mean take me back to the zoo?" said the lemur. "No way, no HOW!"

"Hey, we're going for a happy ending here!" said Skipper.

"But I am happy . . . now," Maurice tried to explain. "I've had it with Julien, he's been a royal pain in my tail for too long! It's all 'Get me this! Get me that!'" he said, impersonating the King. He clenched his fists. "Get me outta there!"

"Kowalski! Reason with him," ordered Skipper.

"Ah, reason . . ." Kowalski stroked his chin thoughtfully for a few seconds before Skipper lost his patience.

"I find reason tedious and boring. Instead we shall use force," he decided.

The penguins grabbed Maurice by the neck and took off, the lemur yelping all the way.

Meanwhile, back at the New York Zoo, King Julien was having a sleepless night. He sat in his throne, munching on a banana and staring miserably at the camera on the ground beneath him. He looked sheepishly into Maurice's terrified, frozen eyes and broke off a piece of banana.

"Here, Maurice, just to show you that I am the bigger lemur." He paused and thought about what he had said. "Not in actual pounds of course, but in the other kind of biggerness. Eat the banana!" He threw the piece graciously at the camera, where it hit the screen and slid to the floor with a squelch.

"Oh," King Julien nodded, knowingly. "So now it's a hunger strike too, is it? You're not going to get me, you know," he said, and started chanting smugly, "you're not going to get me, you're not going to –"

Finally, he broke. "EAT THE BANANA!"

At that moment, the live-action Maurice was not in any position to enjoy a banana. The lemur and the penguins were speeding down the motorway, running on the inside of lorry tyres they'd found in the dump, like four hamsters in their wheels. Maurice was rolling down the road at full-pelt.

"This is insane!" He lost his balance and starting spinning round and round his wheel, totally out of control and screaming wildly.

"Come on, fifth wheel," yelled Skipper, who was now running backwards with ease. "Look sharp!"

There was a tollbooth up ahead with the barrier down, so Rico leapt ahead of the others and quickly regurgitated some change into the machine. The red light flicked to green and the barrier lifted up just in time for the penguins to come rolling through.

The barrier closed before Maurice could reach it, but by now his tyre wasn't rolling – it was bouncing down the road. Luckily for him, it sprung clear over the barrier and he spun off after the others.

After a long while of wheeling, the penguins then dragged Maurice through a manhole in the road and down onto the underground train tracks. They led straight back into the city. The penguins were walking purposefully along the wooden slats between the tracks, but Maurice was again lagging behind.

"Gotta . . . rest!" he wheezed, as he dragged his feet along. His big yellow eyes were drooping with exhaustion, and his brown fur was beginning to look more and more matted and greasy. He really looked like he was about to collapse.

"No dice!" barked Skipper. "We have to be

back at the zoo by 09:00."

"Which does not give us much time," Kowalski deduced.

"We'll just have to go faster," chirruped Private, brightly.

Maurice slumped a little more. "There is no way I can go faster," he whined.

"Oh," said Skipper, putting his flipper around Maurice's shoulders and laughing to himself quietly, "I bet the old D-train will change your tune." He sped off with the other penguins, who easily slid along the rails on their bellies, as if they were made of ice.

Maurice stopped in the middle of the tracks, totally perplexed. "What the –" he started, but an ominous, terrifyingly deep rumble in the tunnel made him pause.

He looked down at the rails. They began to shake and it was only a few seconds before he was shaking too.

As Maurice gulped and looked behind him, two great lights pierced the darkness – a train! And it was charging towards him!

"Oh no!" he screamed and started running as fast as his little legs could carry him.

Back at the zoo, Julien was sitting on his throne, missing Maurice. His eyes fell upon the camera and Maurice's image, which still stared at him with a frozen expression. Julien shifted uncomfortably under the accusing gaze. He leapt off his chair and ran over to the camera.

"Stop looking at me like that!" he screamed,

jumping up and down in frustration. "This is not a contest of staring!" He suddenly stopped, remembering he was supposed to be ignoring Maurice, and turned his back indignantly. "And I am shutting up now because you are still getting 'the shhh treatment'."

He clutched his tail to his chest and tried his hardest not to turn around. His eye started twitching and he grimaced with guilt and desperation. He peeked back – it was too much, and he broke down, falling to the floor.

"I can't take it any more!" he screeched, clutching his head like a lemur on the edge.

"OK, fine! You win! I was wrong about always being right!"

The release was exhausting – Julien's shoulders slumped in defeat, he fell to his knees and hung his head in utter shame. The lemur clutched the camera and shook it desperately, then summoned all his courage for an embarrassing confession. "I-I-I . . . miss you," he whispered, hugging the camera and pressing his cheek against the screen. He was spent. The only remaining course of action was to seek higher help. He had to appeal to the sky spirits. Tilting his head up, his tearful yellow eyes searched the skies above. "OHHHH! I will give anything to get my big-bootied buddy back!"

Meanwhile, Maurice was trying desperately to get his big booty away from a giant speeding train. It was gaining on him, going faster and faster as he felt his chest contract and his breathing become hoarse and laboured. He was not going to make it. His thoughts flew back to his old jungle home and he decided that the fossa that hunted the lemurs seemed like kittens compared to the great beast that was charging at him right now. He had just felt the back of his fur sizzle against the white-hot train lights when a flipper grabbed him by the back of the neck.

He flew upwards, past the train and back onto the sunlit streets of New York. He tottered around for a moment, dazed after his near-death escape, before the penguins pulled him behind a concrete bench.

It was already daybreak and Skipper felt deeply uneasy when he remembered that they had to be back before the zookeeper's morning checks – not to mention the fact they were now out in the open, among humans, and had to proceed with utmost caution.

He and Kowalski peered around the bench through a pair of binoculars. Across the street he saw a group of school children about to board a bus.

"Children," he reported.

"Check," replied Kowalski, spotting the children too.

"Bus."

"Check."

"Zoo brochure."

"Check."

The class teacher was clutching a leaflet for the New York Zoo! The cover featured a picture of Private waving dumbly.

"It's a field trip!" deduced Private, popping his head around to have a look.

The penguins convened behind the bench. Maurice was still staggering around, feeling very dizzy and looking utterly exhausted.

"All right boys, we're almost home. You know what to do," Skipper commanded.

Maurice steadied himself and frowned. What were the penguins planning now?

"Um . . . I don't think I do," he said, confused.

Skipper poked him in the chest with his flipper. Surely Maurice must understand the plan? Now he was just being disobedient.

"Don't get smart with me, soldier. We're not cutting you any slack just because you're the new guy."

The penguins leapt into action. Rico bent down and the penguins used him as a springboard, bouncing off him and over the bench, one by one. Rico looked up at Maurice and raised his eyebrows expectantly – it was his turn. Too slow. Rico couldn't stick around, so he grabbed Maurice around the middle and slung him over the bench.

"Yaaaa!" yelled Maurice as he tore through the air yet again, flying through the open doors of the waiting bus. They were on their way.

In the lemur enclosure, King Julien had taken matters into his own hands. The sky spirits didn't seem to be answering his prayers, so he had determined to break Maurice out of the camera himself. He was tugging at a vine that was attached to a pulley system, slowly raising a huge rock into the air.

"A little to the left!" he shouted at Mort, who was trying to position the camera in the right place under the rock.

"My left or your left?" squeaked the obedient lemur.

"Mine, of course. I am King. The lefts are all mine!" King Julien laughed. "Silly Mort."

But Julien's directions were wrong. Mort moved the camera further and further out of the path of the rock until he was positioned underneath it himself, completely oblivious to his fate. Julien didn't seem to notice his mistake.

Right at that moment, the school bus had stopped outside the zoo and the doors swung open, spitting Maurice out onto the pavement. Skipper bounded out behind him, still bursting with energy.

"Alright, boys. Commence Operation: Shoot the Moon."

The penguins rigged up a giant catapult outside the zoo. A long strip of rubber was pinned to the top of the walls, with a bucket attached in the middle. They pulled the bucket back and back, stretching the rubber tight, and plonked Private inside. Kowalski smacked a helmet onto his head and they let go with a flourish, waiting for him to sail over the walls with ease.

SMACK! Private hit the middle of the wall head-on and slid down it with a groan.

"Three degrees north, Skipper!" he advised, a bit pained.

Maurice was shaking with fear, but the penguins looked completely unconcerned.

"Kowalski! Adjust vector," ordered Skipper. "Rico! Stretcher!" He turned to the horrifed Maurice and slapped him on the back. "Lemur! You're up."

Maurice cowered and shivered, biting his claws in terror. "I can't take it any more! You penguins are psychotic!"

Rico grabbed him around the neck and pulled him towards the bucket.

"Sounds like someone's got a case of the pre-launch heebie-jeebies," laughed Skipper.

Meanwhile, Julien had pulled the vine as far as possible and finally let go. The rock swiftly fell, smacking right on top of Mort and crushing the bewildered lemur into the ground. King Julien looked worried.

"Oh no!" he cried, running towards the rock.

He ran right on past it and knelt in front of the camera. He was more worried about his magic box than the squished lemur. He clutched it and wailed once more in a final act of desperation. "Maurice! I want you back! Come OUT! Great sky spirits, hear my plea!" He covered his weeping eyes with his paws.

Suddenly, a blinding white flash broke Julien out of his stupor and knocked him backwards, as the image on the camera screen was washed into white. The penguins had released Maurice, who had gone soaring high over the top of the zoo walls, descended into the lemur habitat and come to land precisely on top of the camera's shutter release button.

Julien, of course, hadn't seen this. He sat up, blinked, and saw his missing friend splayed on top of the camera. He grinned widely and hugged Maurice's bottom with joy. He thought the sky spirits had finally freed him.

"Maurice!"

"It's good to see you . . . too," replied Maurice, perplexed by Julien's friendliness – he was never this nice. "Look, I'll take you over those crazy –"

"Mission accomplished!" interrupted Skipper smugly, who had safely bounced into the pen behind Maurice.

"Oh!" Julien snapped with his hands on his hips. "As if you had anything to do with it. The sky spirits released Maurice!" He punched the air with his fist. "You rock, sky spirits!"

Skipper looked amused and turned to the old lemur. "Why don't you tell him what really happened, rescued mammal?"

After possibly the worst day of his life spent in the company of the penguins, Maurice had realized Julien wasn't that bad after all. He decided where his loyalties lay and slipped back into his old, obedient self.

"Rule number one: don't question the King," he said, happily.

Skipper smacked his forehead. "Private! Whip me up one of them 'love' smoothies. I need to unwind."

He set off for the penguin pool and waddled past the giant boulder, oblivious to the squeaks coming from beneath it. Maurice and Julien had disappeared, too.

"Guys!" cheeped Mort. "A little help, please? Guys? Guuuuuyyys? . . ."

STORY 3
LAUNCHTIME

It was night in New York City and all was dark, except for the faintly twinkling lights of the Manhattan skyline. A lone grasshopper sung a lullaby and beneath the zoo, the penguins were sleeping peacefully in their lair, curled up in their bunk beds. Skipper was particularly relaxed, snoring loudly, and contentedly dreaming of fish.

Suddenly, a bright ray of light pierced the darkness and flashed across his face. He woke with a start and jumped to attention.

"All hands! Intruder alert!"

The penguins leapt from their beds, flippers poised for action, only to find King Julien and Mort hunched guiltily in front of the mini-fridge in the corner, its electric light shining from the open door. Julien was caught red-handed, mouth full and scouring the fridge for his next snack. Mort was guzzling juice straight from the carton.

"Hello, neighbour," screeched Julien, merrily.

"Hey!" yelled Skipper, his flippers on his hips in angry disbelief. "Those snack provisions are for authorized personnel only!"

Julien wagged his finger at the penguin leader, raising himself to his full height.

"Do not worry, it is only I, King Julien, who is borrowing your delicious food for my stomach." He pulled a huge iced sponge cake from the fridge and patted his belly happily. "Yes," he emphasized, as he walked towards Skipper, "that is it: borrowing."

Skipper growled quietly, annoyed.

The next morning, the penguins were up early and ready for action. They were outside beside the penguin pool, training hard at their karate moves. Skipper was concentrating, leading them through their routine.

"Hiiiii-ya! And kick, punch, and chop. Ha! Duck, spin, and backward!"

The penguins moved in unison, a dizzying flurry of legs and tails. They were finding their groove; a lean, mean, fighting machine. They thrust forward for their final impressive move.

"And . . ."

BAM! A golf ball had flown towards them, thwacking Private on the head. He staggered around dizzily for a moment, twirling on one toe, before collapsing in a heap, face-first. The penguins looked up to see Julien, golf club in hand a few metres away, waving at them gaily. Mort was teeing up another golf ball.

"Hello, neighbour!" he shouted, and took a big swing, hitting the ball towards them. "Fore!"

Skipper caught the ball. He frowned and growled, his cheeks turning a deep shade of red. This was the second time in twenty-four hours those lemurs had disturbed their peace and quiet! He refused to shout – that would show he'd lost control in front of his team. As his rage bubbled away inside him, he crushed the golf ball to a powder with his flipper.

"It is OK," grinned Julien, unworried, "I have 400 more golf balls where that came from!" He pointed towards a huge pile.

"I like golf!" squeaked Mort, as he teed up

yet another ball, staring up adoringly at

Julien took a swing, missed the ball
Mort instead.

"I like flying!" sang the lemur, as he s......
towards Skipper, bounced off his head, and
landed in the penguin pool with a splash.

"I don't like drowning . . ." he gurgled sadly,
as he sank to the bottom.

Skipper closed his eyes and sighed. He was
fast losing patience with his lemur neighbours.

That evening, Skipper had shaken off his
frustration and settled down to a game of
chess with Kowalski. The penguins were sat
comfortably on the ground, making approving
'hmms' and 'ahhhs' as each took their turn to
play. Skipper studied the board carefully, as he
considered his next move. His brow furrowed
and his finger hovered over his queen. He
smiled, certain he was just about to move her
to certain victory, when a loud siren made him
jump, sending the precious chess piece flying.

The penguins looked over to see King Julien
making himself at home in front of their TV, a
police show blaring from the speakers.

"Look out! Coming through," said Maurice
behind them, clutching a huge box of popcorn
and barging right across the chessboard,
knocking a few more pieces out of the way. He
plonked himself down next to Julien in front of
the TV. They were clearly intending on being
there for a long session.

"What the –" started Skipper, but the

enguins barely had time to open their beaks before Mort crash-landed on the board, toppling the remaining pieces over and ruining the game once and for all.

"You've run out of juice," he advised helpfully, brandishing an empty carton.

Skipper had finally had enough. He waddled angrily over to Julien and started shouting at him. "This is our home, our H.Q., our inner sanctum, you can't just –"

But Julien slowly turned up the volume on the TV set until Skipper was drowned out entirely.

"I can't hear you!" yelled Julien, pointing at his ear. "TV too loud!"

Just then, Skipper felt a sharp knock to the head. He turned to see Mort head-spinning happily on the chessboard, his tail flicking pieces into the air. A bishop whizzed past his ear.

Skipper stared at him. His left eye started twitching. The fury built slowly in his belly and he could feel it rising like hot lava. His whole body began to shake as he tightened his fists, growled deeply, and then let out an almighty, explosive roar that echoed through the night. Enough was enough. His patience with the lemurs had finally run out!

The next day, Skipper called a penguin meeting in the lair. He looked very serious as he paced back and forth, his hands clasped behind his back. The other penguins waited expectantly, knowing that Skipper was about to deliver something important.

"Gentlemen," he announced decidedly, "we need a vacation . . . a vacation from that lemur!"

Private hopped forward. "We could visit a zoo!" he piped excitedly, producing a leaflet. His grin spread and his little beady eyes shone. "They have pandas and hippos and a lovely house of reptiles –"

"Private," interrupted Skipper, "you do know we live in a zoo?"

"But we could visit a different zoo!" he offered, undiscouraged.

On the nod from Skipper, Rico gave him a slap over the head.

"Kowalski! Calculate the farthest trip possible from our present location," he barked. Kowalski started furiously tapping away at the keys to a large computer.

"Climate?" asked Kowalski.

"Unspecified," answered Skipper.

"Elevation?"

"Unimportant."

"Lemur population?"

Skipper narrowed his eyes. "Zero point zero per cent," he spat.

"I've come up with two vacations within our location parameters," he announced finally.

Skipper walked over and looked at the screen. "I can't set foot in Denmark," he said.

"Why not?" asked Private.

"That's private, Private," he answered mysteriously and looked into the distance. "Between me and the Danes."

That left only one location. Kowalski tapped

a few more keys and the computer displayed the result. Skipper turned back to his team.

"Gentlemen, we're going . . . to the moon!"

Rico and Private gasped in shock.

"And no," he added, before Private could ask, "there is no zoo on the moon."

Over the next few days, the penguins busied themselves making preparations for their grand voyage and Kowalski got to work on the rocket.

Soon enough, everything was ready and the time for lift-off had arrived. The penguins kitted themselves out in homemade spacesuits and helmets and Skipper led them outside to stand at the foot of their new craft.

"Men, I present to you: *The Penguin One*," said Skipper, dramatically.

They gazed up. The rocket towered above them impressively, but on closer inspection seemed to be made up of old scavenged zoo rubbish and didn't exactly look flight-worthy.

"Is it . . . safe?" asked Private, unsure, as a piece of trash can unhinged itself and crashed to the ground.

"Technically speaking . . ." said Kowalski, "maybe."

Skipper ushered them onboard. He would be co-pilot, of course, and sat himself next to Kowalski near the control panel. Private and Rico belted up in the back seats, ready for take-off.

"Say goodbye to Earth, boys."

83

"But Skipper," said Private timidly, gripping the edge of the circular window and gazing dejectedly out at the zoo. "Earth has some of my favourite things . . . like cookies and . . . oxygen!"

"And brown paper packages tied up in string," mocked Skipper. No one was stopping this trip now – he had to take a break from those lemurs. "Kowalski!" he shouted. "Light this candle!"

Kowalski flipped a switch on the console, which lit the fuse to a huge pile of Rico's dynamite sticks, packed under the rocket. He began the count down. "T minus five, four, three, two, one . . ."

The crackle of the approaching spark grew closer. Private gulped, grasped his seat, and looked to Rico for reassurance. He was fast asleep.

"Ignition!" shouted Kowalski.

Ka-boom! The dynamite erupted, and the craft blasted off from the launch pad in a cloud of thick black smoke. Burning orange flame catapulted it up, up, into the night sky.

On a nearby rooftop, a plump grey pigeon was perched on an antenna. He watched the rocket streak past, before turning to a scrawny alley cat, who was trying to creep up behind him. The bird looked totally unfazed.

"Yo, Max! Do I look a little chunkier to you?" the bird teased, fluffing his wings. "I mean, I've been exercising, but no matter how I try, I can't get rid of all this succulent, delicious, dark MEAT!"

The pigeon wiggled his fat bottom at the cat. Max was transfixed by the podgy, juicy-looking rump. He dribbled and quivered with excitement and took a flying leap at it.

But the pigeon dodged and flew sideways just in time, leaving Max soaring over the side of the building. He managed to grasp the edge of the rooftop as he fell, and dangled there, clinging on for dear life with his claws.

The pigeon leered down at him. "Give it up, hairball!" he jeered. "You've never caught a bird in your life. Never have, never will!" He cackled and flew off, his tempting rear disappearing in the distance.

Max heaved himself up over the ledge and sprawled on his back, defeated. He was so hungry. He held his grumbling stomach and looked wistfully up into the night sky. He wasn't having any success trying to get a decent meal on his own. What he needed was a little help. Or a stroke of luck. No – a miracle.

"Wow!" he exclaimed, as he saw a trail of light. "A shooting star!" Now was his chance! He could wish for something truly amazing. "I wish . . . I wish . . . for a bird that can't fly away!"

The shooting star got larger and larger as he gazed at it, dreaming of his imaginary bird supper. Wait – that was no shooting star, it was the penguins' rocket, speeding headlong towards him! He leapt out of its path and jumped into an air-conditioning shaft as it scraped across the rooftop in a shower of sparks and skidded to a halt in a heap.

Back at the zoo, the lemurs were up to their usual tricks. King Julien, Maurice and Mort crept towards the penguins' lair and Julien popped his head around the door.

"Hello, neighbours?" he called, tiptoeing inside. "I would like to borrow your toothbrushes to scrub my hard-to-reach regions. If you agree, say nothing at all . . ."

Silence.

"I guess they agree," shrugged Maurice.

Julien stepped forward and accidentally trod on a remote control. A tinny voice started babbling enthusiastically behind them, "This is a once-in-a-lifetime opportunity!"

The lemurs turned slowly to look at the giant TV, its glorious colours and sounds calling them to misbehave. Julien smiled craftily and gestured at it.

"And as long as we are borrowing, how about a little television, Maurice?"

The old lemur looked worried. "You mean BIG television . . . big and heavy."

Julien paused for a moment. "You know," he mused, "my brain is now saying that the King, which is me, should not have to lift heavy things."

They both turned to look at Mort.

Ever anxious to please, his little eyes brightened. "I like heavy lifting!" he cheeped.

Just a rooftop away, the penguins emerged from their battered rocket, their heads covered with huge homemade space helmets. It was dark and a thick fog had descended around them.

"Welcome to the moon, boys", said Skipper, thinking their voyage had taken them out of the atmosphere, as planned. Little did he know they were only one building away from home. He peered through the smoke. They couldn't see much at all. "Lemur population: zip, zero, nada. Beautiful!"

Kowalski was punching buttons on his handheld 'tricorder', taking samples of the atmosphere. The little machine beeped and buzzed. "Oxygen reading: surprisingly high," he said, confused.

Rico was nearby, trying to lick the ground through his helmet. Kowalski bent down and examined the surface. "Hmmm. Moon cheese content: surprisingly low." Rico whined.

"Private," Skipper instructed the flag-wielding penguin, "claim this rock in the name of –"

"Penguins!" exclaimed Max the cat, out of earshot. He was peeking out from the air conditioning tube. "How did penguins get up here when they –" he paused and gasped in excited realization, "CAN'T FLY?!" He jumped up excitedly and bashed his head, sending him tumbling, screeching and banging down the metal shaft.

The penguins, alert as ever, whipped around when they heard the noise.

"I'm picking up a possible alien life form," warned Kowalski seriously, as he consulted his tricorder.

The penguins leapt together in fighting stance.

"Game on, boys," said Skipper. "Disperse and investigate!"

Skipper, Kowalski and Rico zipped off at lightning speed, leaving Private, always a step behind, standing confused and alone.

"Skipper?" he called softly, waddling around blindly in the mist. "Hello? Aliens?" Out of the corner of his eye, he saw something streak past him. Gulp.

As he moved further into the fog, Max was creeping up behind him. The hungry cat was just about to pounce when Private spotted something on the ground and plunged to pick it up. "A moon rock!" he exclaimed. He looked closer. "Oh. It's just a baseball . . ." he began, disappointed again, before realizing this baseball was pretty special, "that flew all the way to the moon!"

Max raised his arms to try and strike again, just as Private threw the ball in the air with joy. It fell over his shoulder, clunking Max on the head.

Private turned to see the mangy cat, spread-eagled behind him. "Oh! Hello," said Private.

Max perked up immediately at the sight of his potential dinner. "Ha hee hee!" he chuckled gleefully. "Greetings, my little friend!" He pulled himself up. "Excuse me . . . are you . . . a penguin?"

"Why yes, I am," said Private, simply.

Max rubbed his paws together in anticipation. "A flightless bird! That means no flapping, no flying, no . . . resistance." He almost

choked on his own hysterical laughter. Who needed that fat pigeon now? This bird couldn't fly away! He patted the little penguin's helmet and looked at him, hungrily.

Private looked back, dumbly. What was this creature talking about?

"Kudos, Private," interrupted Skipper, as he appeared out of the fog with the other penguins. "You've discovered an alien life form."

Max could barely believe his eyes. "Four of them," he said greedily. "A buffet!" He ran towards Skipper and slipped on the discarded baseball, sliding to land at the penguins' feet.

Kowalski eyed Max sceptically. "Skipper, this alien is oddly cat-like in structure."

"A moon cat, eh?" he answered.

Max's eyes burst open. "Moon cat?" he asked, confused.

"Greetings, Moon Cat," continued Skipper. "We come in peace. For now. Sometimes Rico can't help himself." Rico nodded, a little insanely.

"You really think you're on the moon?" said Max, perplexed. This was ridiculous.

"Affirmative," said Kowalski.

The cat considered this for a second. A plan started to form.

"Well, good . . . because you are! Definitely. You're on the moon. Welcome!"

The sound of distant sirens and the whirring blades of an approaching helicopter suddenly made him jump with fright. "Uh oh," he panicked, as a searchlight from the helicopter started sweeping back and forth across the rooftop, inching closer to them every time. He couldn't let the penguins be discovered – they were too precious!

"They spotted your crash. They'll want to take you away!" trembled Max.

"Who exactly is 'they'?" asked Skipper.

Max had to think fast. "The . . . uh . . . evil Moon Warriors!" He leapt behind the penguins and tried to usher them away from the light.

Skipper looked unfazed. "We can take 'em!" Rico growled affirmatively.

"But, but," jabbered Max. He had to convince them to hide, and quickly! "That beam is their Death Ray!"

"Death Ray?" scoffed Skipper. "Pfft. Bring it on." The penguins snapped into karate positions, ready for a fight.

Max was at his wit's end. "Look, I refuse to let anything happen to you guys. You're coming with me." He grabbed the penguins and bustled them into his hut, narrowly escaping the swooping beam of light.

"And to think he just met us," smiled Private, happily. This 'Moon Cat' was so polite!

Meanwhile, standing in the penguins' lair, King Julien and Maurice were watching Mort desperately trying to push the huge TV all by himself. It hadn't budged an inch.

Julien looked a little sympathetic. "Poor Mort," he said, walking over, "let me help you." He leaned in close to the lemur. "LIFT WITH YOUR LEGS!" he exploded in his ear. "YOUR TINY, TINY LEGS!"

He hopped up and down, intensely frustrated.

"I'm . . . trying," wheezed Mort, painfully.

Maurice was looking around suspiciously. He rubbed his chin. "You know, your majesty, I thought for sure the penguins would have this place booby-trapped."

Just then, Mort finally managed to shift the TV a miniscule amount, and the lemurs heard a 'click' as a fish trophy mounted on the wall popped open, revealing a hidden opening. A booby trap! Half a dozen forks shot rapid fire from the hole.

King Julien jumped clear, leaving Mort pinned to the wall, wide-eyed and completely surrounded by cutlery. He let out a terrified yelp.

"Mort," said Julien, poking the little lemur's stomach, "I'm starting to think you're not taking this job seriously."

Julien fingered the edge of the TV. Perhaps if he just tried to move it a little . . . he gave it a nudge and a huge plastic washing basket fell from above, trapping him and Mort inside.

"Agh! Maurice!" he squawked.

Maurice ran over to them and tugged at the basket. It began to tip and then rolled over and over across the floor, finally spitting the lemurs out in a heap. Julien jumped to his feet, jubilantly.

"Ha, ha!" he laughed, just as another basket clamped shut over them.

Back on the rooftop, the penguins were sitting around a table in Max's makeshift hut. He'd given them some rainwater drinks in old cans and

cartons and was now furtively sharpening a knife in the corner.

"Moon Cat," said Skipper, "I'm touched by your hospitality."

"Yeah," said Max sarcastically, as he looked at as his knife and fork. He turned around and held up his weapons with glee. "Well! It's time to eat!" he chuckled maniacally.

"Now he's making us a meal!" said Private. The penguins really hadn't cottoned on. "You, sir, are a model of kindness."

Max licked his lips and slipped his hand behind his back. Out of view, he knocked on the side of a wooden box. "Oh, my!" he said, putting his hand to his mouth and pretending to be afraid of the make-believe aliens. "Do you hear that? They're coming! You'd better use my teleportation machine to hide." He pointed to an old, battered microwave in the corner of the room. If he could convince the penguins to jump inside, his dinner would be ready in no time!

"Teleportation?" said Kowalski, his arms crossed doubtingly. "That's pure science fiction!"

Max thought on his feet. "Which is exactly why I have to disguise it as a microwave oven! It's top secret."

Kowalski looked impressed. "Camouflage. Well-played."

Private waddled over to the oven and tried to crawl inside it. Bonk! His helmet was too big to fit through the door. He kept banging his head against it regardless, determined to get inside. Max picked him up angrily and started thwacking him against the opening, desperately trying to force him in.

"Bit of a squeeze," said Private, disappointed.

"Maybe if you took off the helmet . . ." said Max, still straining to force the penguin inside.

Skipper, Rico and Kowalski watched appreciatively from the table.

"This moon cat has opened his home, his heart, and his top-secret technology to us," said Kowalski.

Rico grunted in agreement.

"Ten four on that!" added Skipper. "He's downright neighbourly!" He paused for a moment and thought suddenly of his own neighbours, the lemurs. Was he as kind to them? He looked back over the incidents of the past few days; the fridge, the golf, the TV. No. He hadn't been particularly patient with them. And certainly not very neighbourly. He felt guilty.

"You know, Kowalski," he said, "maybe I need to sign on to Moon Cat's good neighbour policy."

They looked over at the cat, who was now trying to shove Private into the microwave with a plunger. The plunger sucked and clamped firm to Private's bottom. Max held it aloft. "Forget the microwave!" he screamed in frustration.

"You mean teleportation device," said Private, helpfully.

"Whatever!" screeched the cat, hurling the plunger, and Private with it, to the floor. He loomed over him. "No more fooling around." His breathing was ragged and desperate. "It's time!" He raised his claws.

Before he could strike, Skipper stepped in front of Private to shake Max's paw.

"Moon Cat is so right!" he said, gratefully. "We can't fool around on the moon any longer. It is time. Time to go home!" Skipper ushered Private towards the door.

Max stood in disbelief. These penguins were impossible! "Wait . . . What? . . . Nooooooo!" He fell to his knees, crying and wailing. He'd lost his second chance at dinner that night. He really was a useless excuse for a cat.

"Thanks for everything, Moon Cat," said Skipper. "Rico! Gift him."

Rico lifted his helmet and spat out a tin of sardines, which landed right in front of Max's nose. He blinked his tears away and stared at the fish in utter shock.

"Food? For me?" He gobbled down a sardine, savouring the first taste of proper food he'd had in a long time. "No one's ever, ever, given me a gift before!" He clutched his face, overcome with emotion.

"You're quite welcome," said Skipper.

The penguins made their way back to *The Penguin One* and buckled up for the ride home. Kowalski started up the engine and Private waved happily out of the window at Max, who had come to see them off, still clutching his tinned fish.

The rocket blasted off and climbed skyward. Within seconds, it started to shake, shudder and groan. Skipper glanced sideways at Kowalski, who was furiously tapping away at the control panel, and asked for a status report.

"I am randomly pushing buttons as we spin out of control, Skipper," he answered, seriously.

Skipper gulped. "Can I push one? I'd feel better."

In the back seats, Private gripped his arm-rests, wide-eyed and terrified, while Rico snored, peacefully asleep again.

The rocket tipped and began to plummet head-first towards the zoo at breakneck speed.

"Prepare for splash-down," advised Kowalski, as he aimed the craft at the penguin pool, hoping for a soft landing.

SMACK! They missed it entirely and landed on the concrete, a pile of tangled metal and fumes.

"Or . . . crash-down, as it were."

The penguins popped up out of the wreckage, miraculously unharmed. Skipper squeezed off his helmet and peered through the smoke. He thought he'd spotted something odd. He shook his head and blinked. He blinked again. No, his eyes weren't deceiving him. Straight ahead were the lemurs, trapped in a basket, pushing the penguins' TV across the ground.

Julien spotted him and waved guiltily. "Ah . . . hello, trap-happy penguins! We were just 'borrowing' your –" He broke off. "It was Mort's idea!" He pointed at his little helper.

"Uh-oh!" squeaked Mort.

Skipper looked at them and broke into a grin. "Not to worry, my ring-tailed neighbour," he announced brightly, as Rico and Kowalski tipped the basket sideways to free the trapped lemurs. "I've had a little attitude adjustment thanks to my visit up there . . ." He gestured at the moon glowing in the night sky. Everyone gazed up in wonder at the mysterious place they had just visited, nestled between curls of mist and twinkling stars.

Just then, a helicopter beam slashed across their view. It fixed on a nearby rooftop, just metres away from where they stood, shining directly on Max, who waved, merrily gobbling his tin of sardines. The moon glowed behind him, millions more miles away.

"Thanks for the fish!" Max yelled.

Skipper furrowed his brow and turned slowly to face Kowalski.

"So . . . we didn't go lunar?"

Kowalski whipped out his calculator. "Hmm, it seems I forgot to carry the two."

"And there's no such thing as moon cat hospitality?" asked Skipper, his smile fading.

Rico shook his head.

Skipper paused, then frowned in thought. The penguins hadn't discovered anything at all – in fact, nothing had changed. The moon was a rooftop, the 'Moon Cat' was an alley cat, and the lemurs were nothing but pesky thieves. He whipped around to face the ring-tailed rascals, and his TV.

"Looks like we have intruders, boys. Commence Operation: Hammer Head!"

The penguins glared at their light-fingered enemies.

"Excuse me, hammer whose head, exactly?" asked Julien, raising his finger.

Rico pulled out a hammer, his eyes flashing menacingly.

"Arghhhhh!" yelped Julien.

The lemurs fled, screaming, followed closely by the penguins, leaping ninja-style into the air, brandishing the hammer.

After the penguins' holiday, everything was back to normal: the lemurs and the penguins would live to have another neighbourly battle!

HAPPY KING
JULIEN DAY
AND OTHER STORIES

COLLECT THESE OTHER FANTASTIC TITLES:

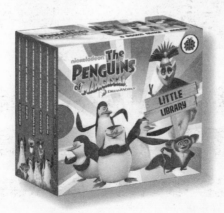